For Lulu's new little brother Ben, and for Naked Babies everywhere!

THIS IS A BORZOI BOOK PUBLISHED BY ALFRED A. KNOPF

Copyright © 2007 by Maggie Smith

Published in the United States by Alfred A. Knopf, an imprint of Random House Children's Books,
a division of Random House, Inc., New York.

KNOPF, BORZOI BOOKS, and the colophon are registered trademarks of Random House, Inc.

www.randomhouse.com/kids

Educators and librarians, for a variety of teaching tools, visit us at www.randomhouse.com/teachers

Library of Congress Cataloging-in-Publication Data
Smith, Maggie.
One naked baby : counting to ten and back again / Maggie Smith. — 1st ed.
p. cm.
SUMMARY: Illustrations and simple rhymes go from one to ten and back again over the course of a baby's day.
ISBN 978-0-375-83329-8 (trade) — ISBN 978-0-375-93329-5 (lib. bdg.)
[1. Babies—Fiction. 2. Counting. 3. Stories in rhyme.] I. Title.
PZ8.3.S6544On 2007   [Fic]—dc22 2006016078

The illustrations in this book were created using watercolor paints.

MANUFACTURED IN CHINA

February 2007

10 9 8 7 6 5 4 3 2 1
First Edition

One Naked Baby

MAGGIE SMITH

COUNTING TO TEN AND BACK AGAIN

ALFRED A. KNOPF · NEW YORK

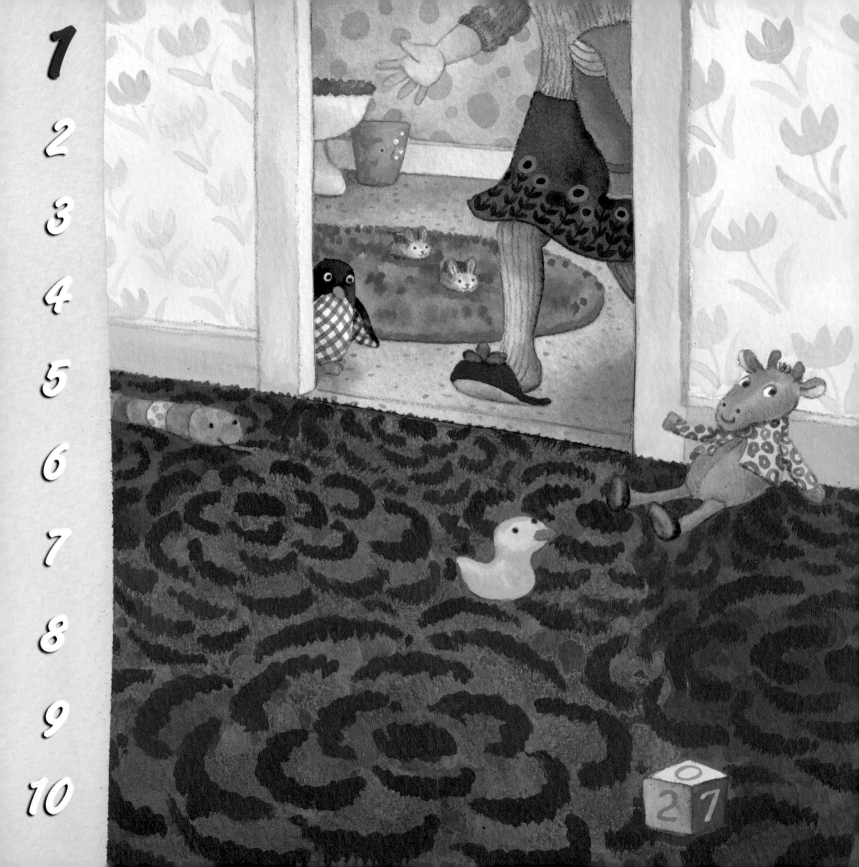

1
2
3
4
5
6
7
8
9
10

ONE naked baby,

1
2
3
4
5
6
7
8
9
10

TWO fat cats,

THREE laundry baskets,

1
2
3
4
5
6
7
8
9
10

FOUR silly hats!

FIVE toes for tickling,

1
2
3
4
5
6
7
8
9
10

SIX crunchy fish.

SEVEN bunny cookies on a purple-flowered dish.

1
2
3
4
5
6
7
8
9
10

EIGHT shiny buttons,

1
2
3
4
5
6
7
8
9
10

NINE tiny chicks.

"Out!" says Baby, and the doorknob clicks.

1
2
3
4
5
6
7
8
9
10

What's waiting for Baby, so yellow and bright?

TEN happy daffodils—oh, what a sight!

NINE stones for stepping,

1
2
3
4
5
6
7
8
9
10

EIGHT robins race,

1
2
3
4
5
6
7
8
9
10

SEVEN worms wiggle,

SIX
chipmunks
chase.

FIVE sturdy sticks that Baby picks up,

1
2
3
4
5
6
7
8
9
10

FOUR perfect puddles,

1
2
3
4
5
6
7
8
9
10

THREE wet pups!

1
2
3
4
5
6
7
8
9
10

TWO muddy froggy boots splash up the path—

1
2
3
4
5
6
7
8
9
10

and **ONE** naked baby goes back in the bath!

1
2
3
4
5
6
7
8
9
10